Goodnight Fox

Yap Yap

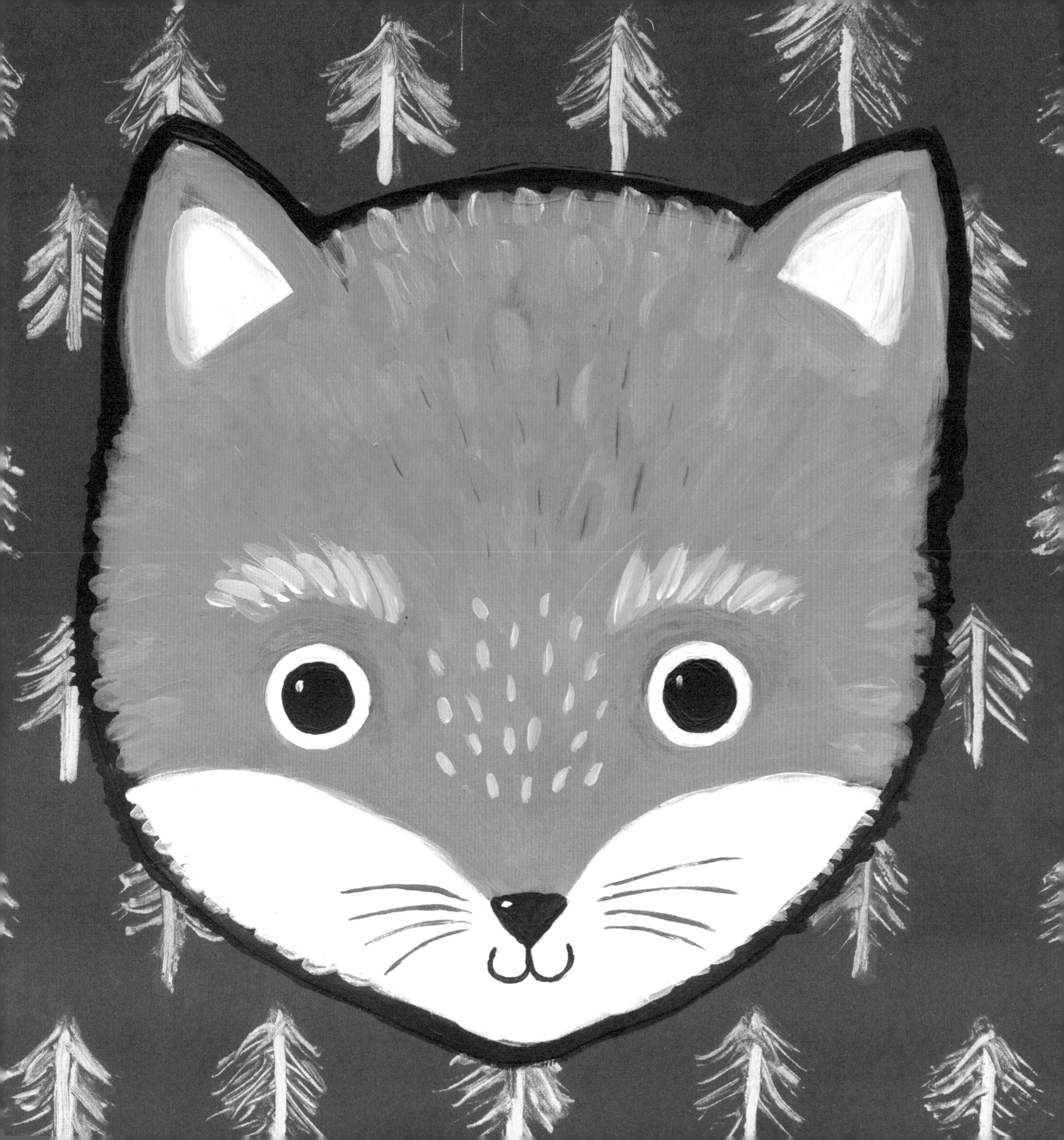

Goodnight Owl Twit Twoo

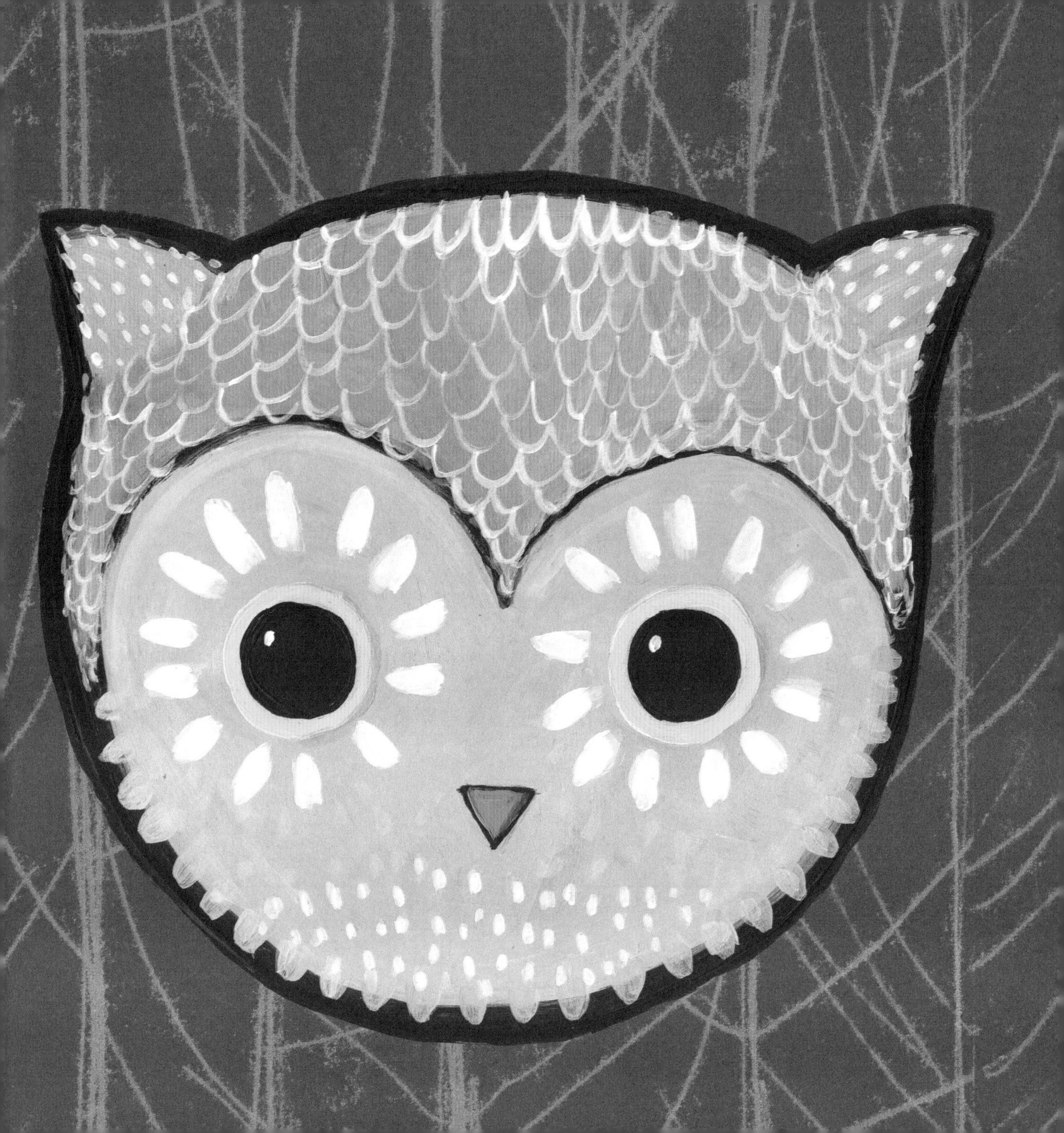

Goodnight Bat

Flap Flap

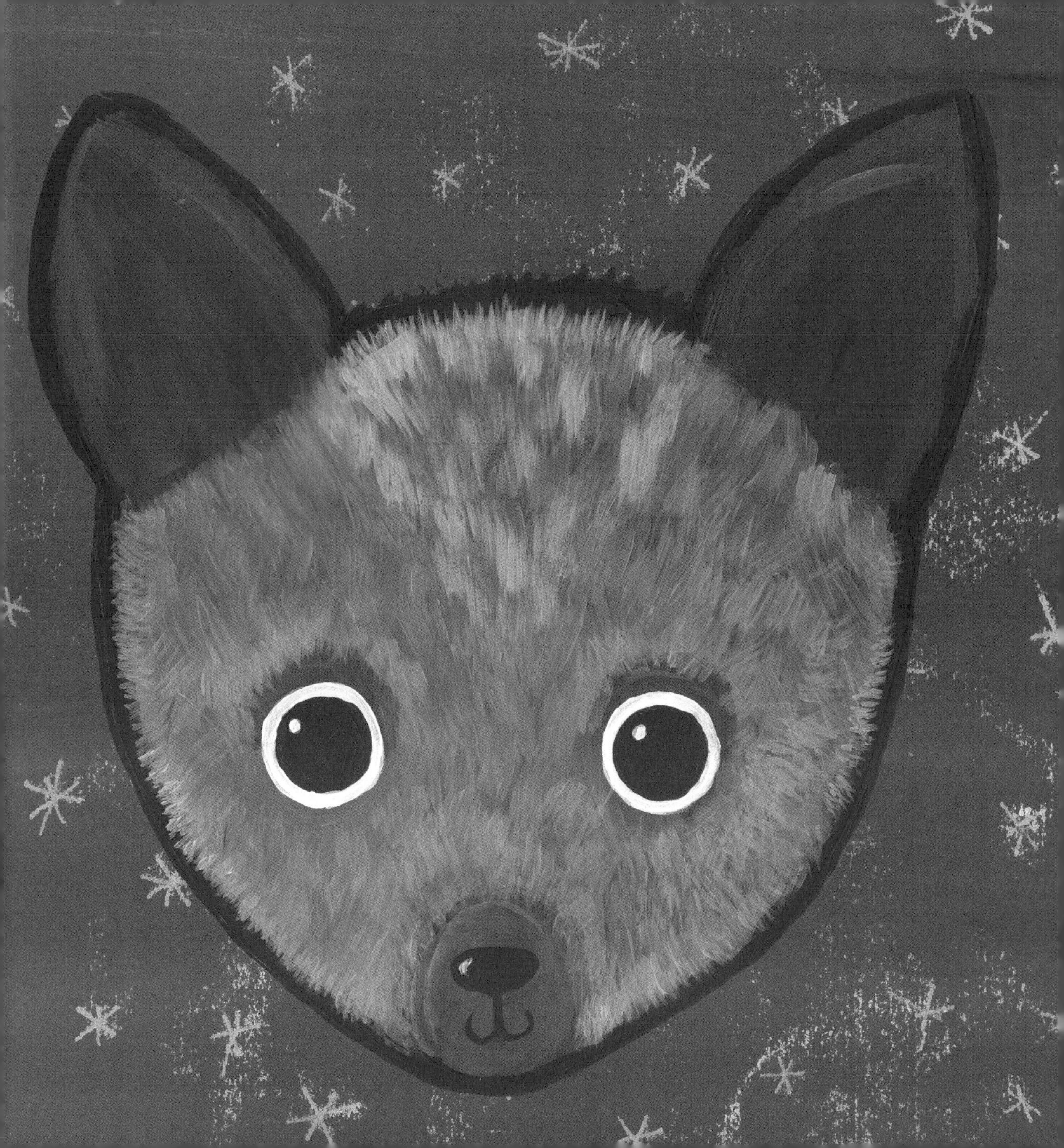

Goodnight Mouse
Squeak Squeak

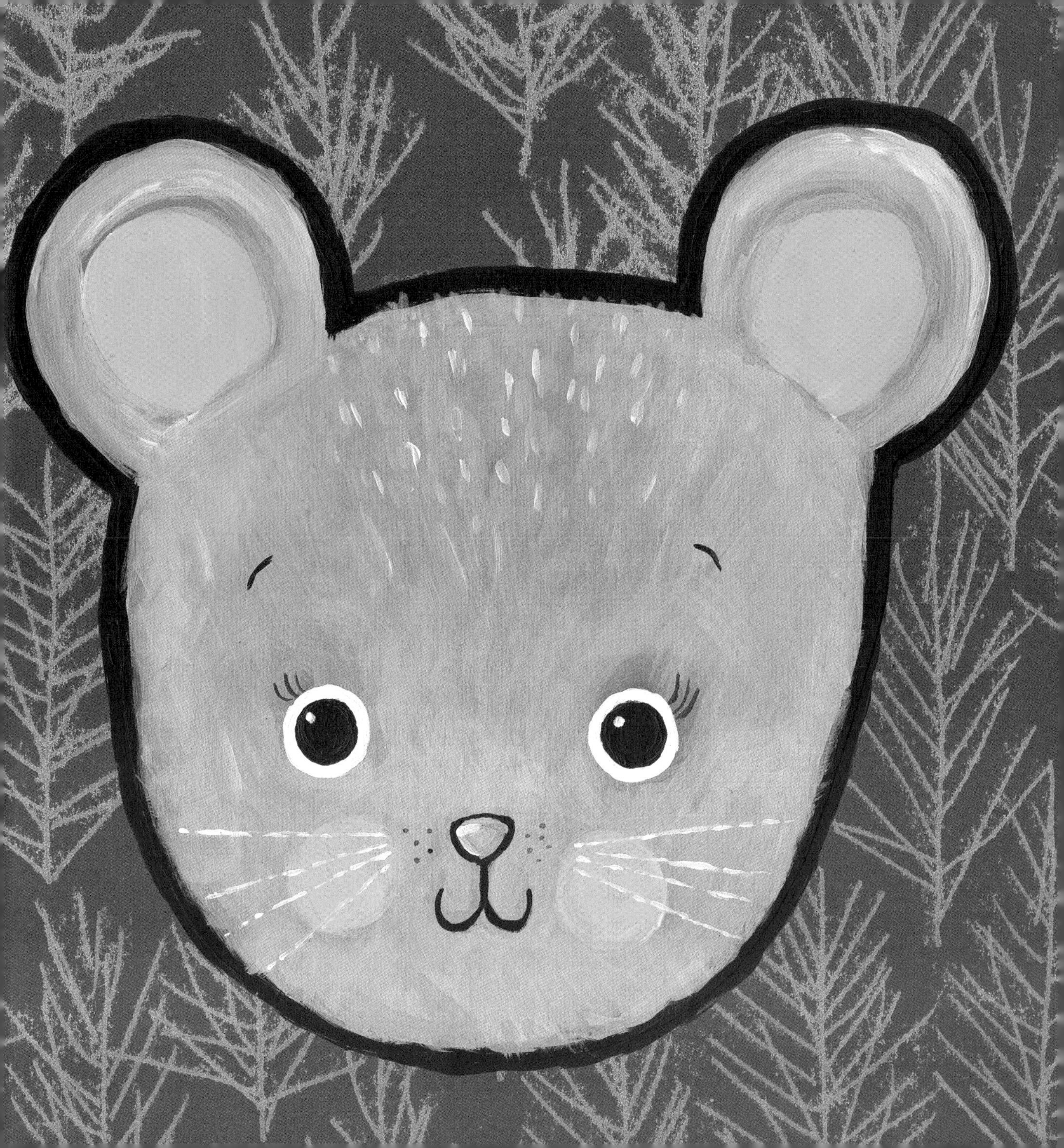

Goodnight Kitten

Meow Meow

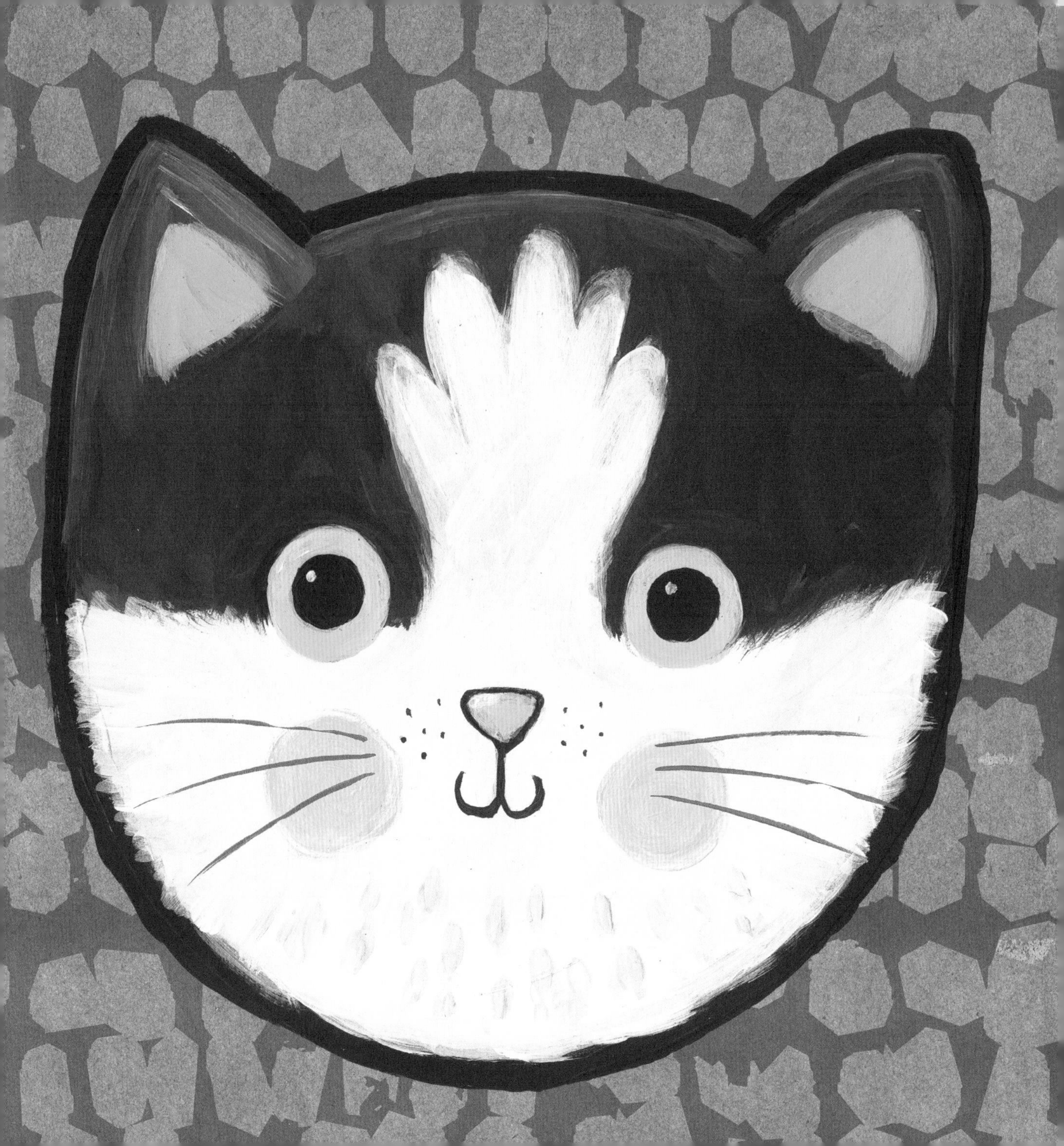

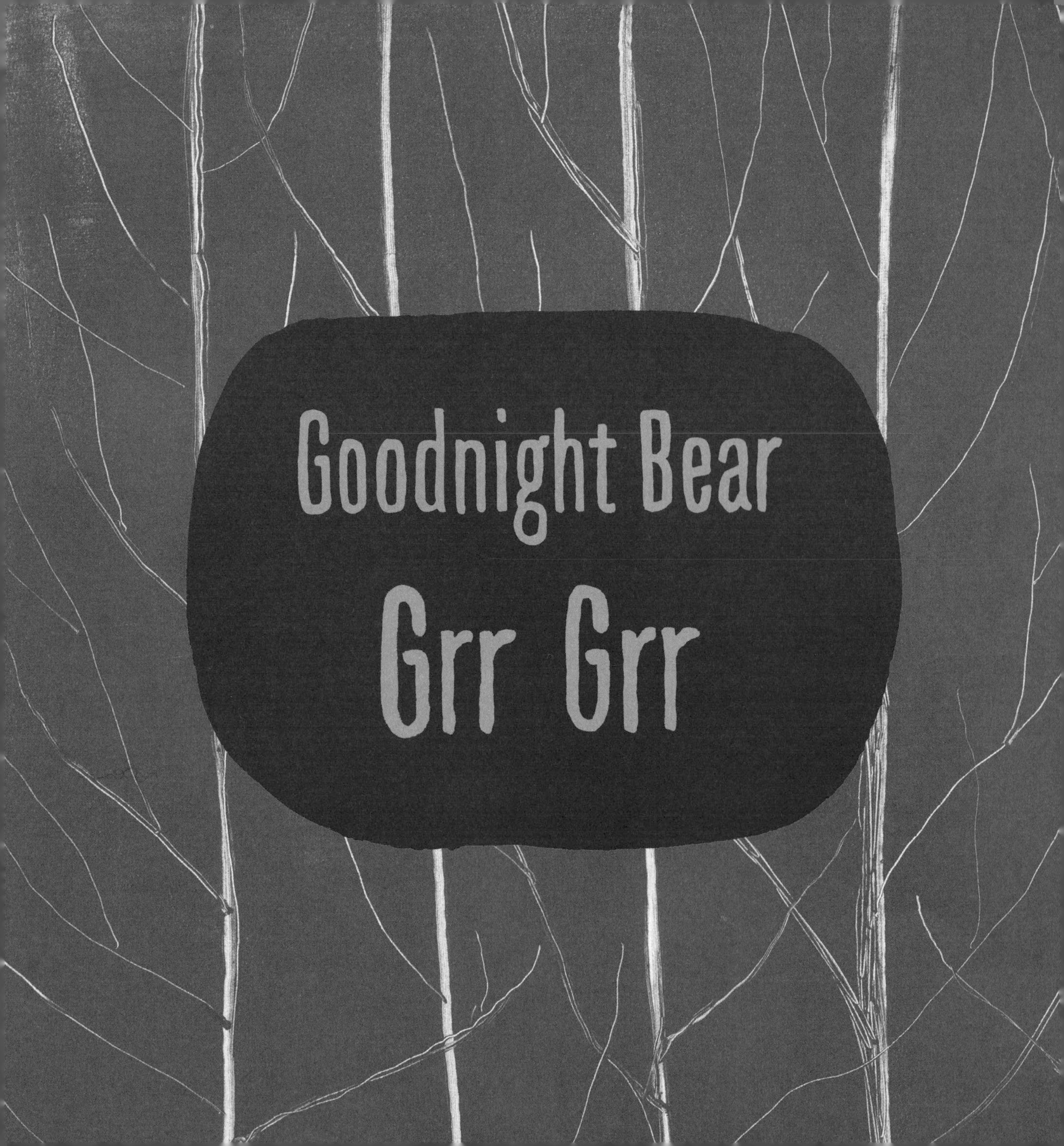
Goodnight Bear
Grr Grr

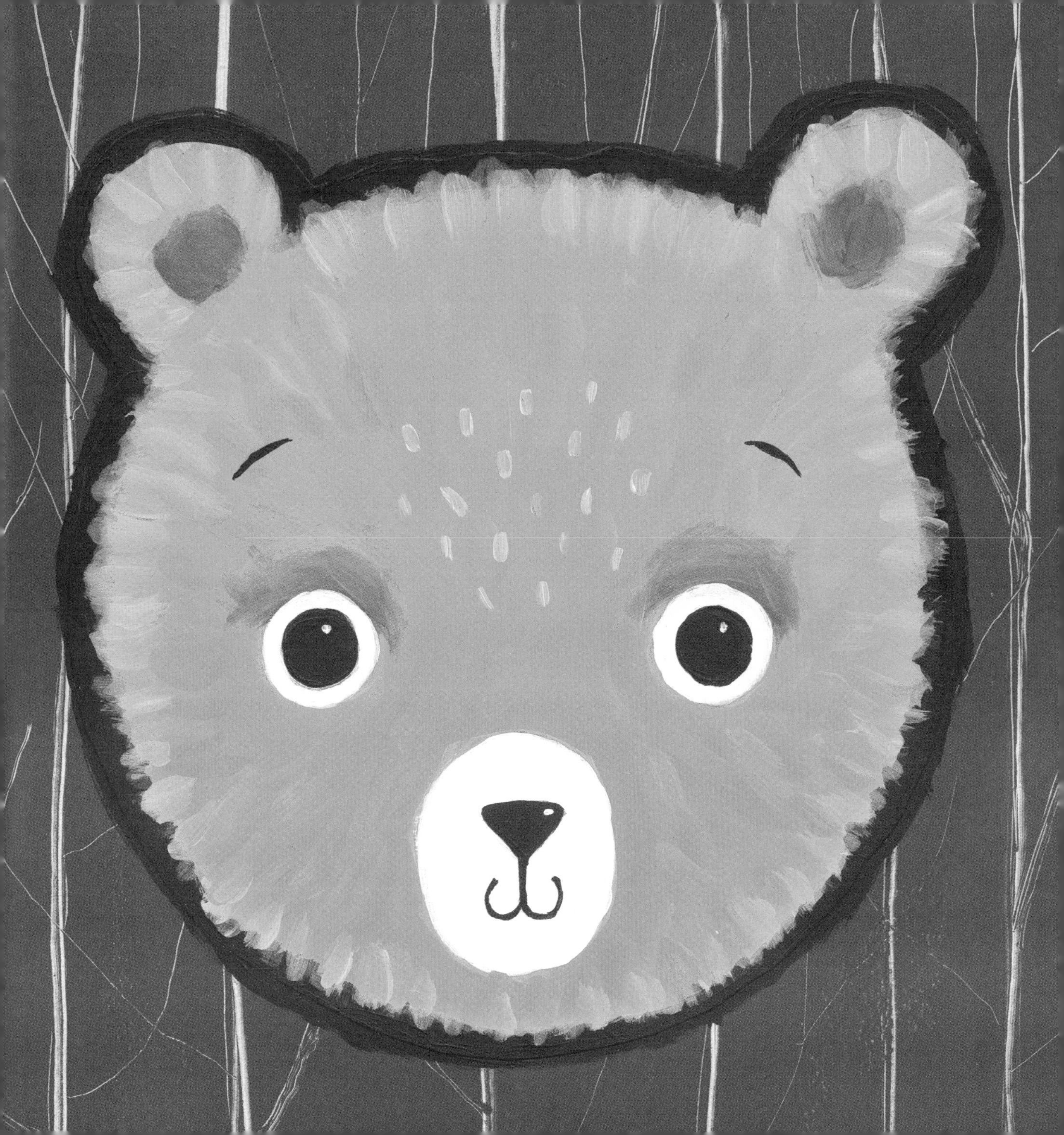

Goodnight Hedgehog
Snuffle Snuffle

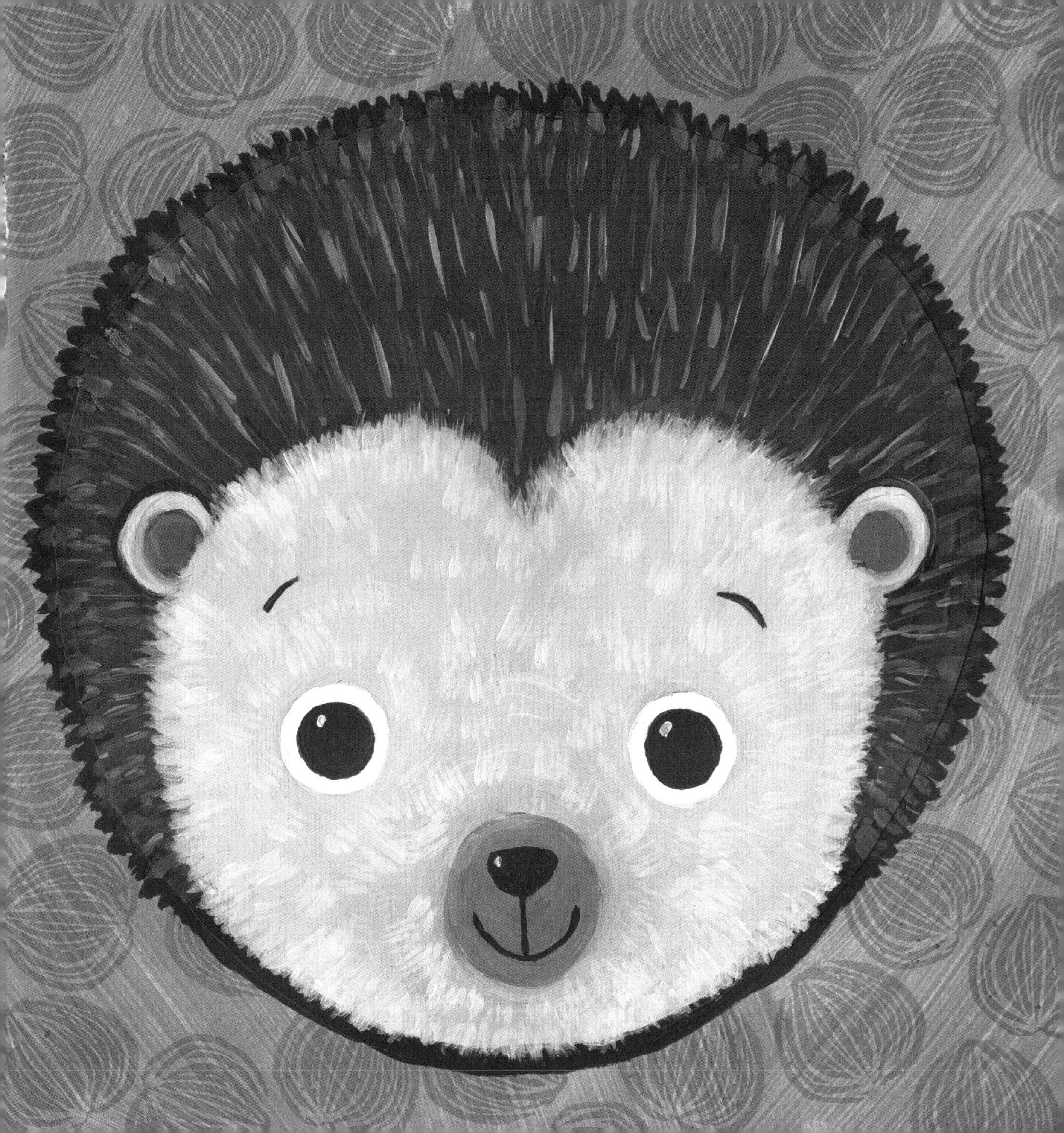

Goodnight Wolf

Wooh Wooh